# the slaughterhouse poems

# dave newman

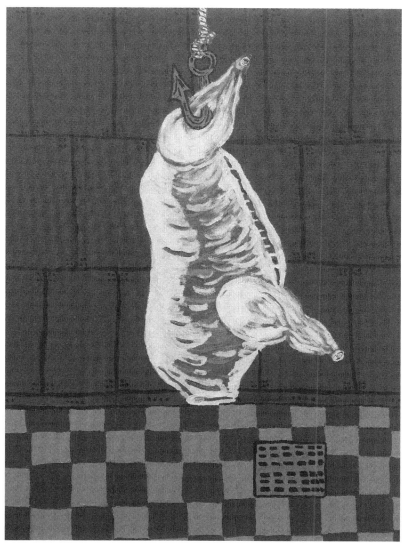

*Steer Painting by Lou Ickes*

Copyright ©2013 by Dave Newman
All rights reserved.

Published by White Gorilla Press
186 Waterview Avenue
Belford, NJ 07718

Visit us at www.whitegorillapress.com

Cover design by Dan Rugh

These poems are works of fiction. Any resemblance to actual persons, living or dead, is entirely coincidental.

No part of this book can be reproduced in any medium without the written permission of the publisher.

ISBN: 0988445913
ISBN-13: 9780988445918

This book is dedicated to Lou Ickes
great friend
excellent painter
bartender extraordinaire
rock 'n' roll genius
and Turkey Bowl MVP circa 1995

Let's get together around 8 or 8:30

I'm waiting for a letter with good news
maybe it will arrive the day I die
but it will come for sure

-Nazim Hikmet


Jesus hates you

-Jimmy Cvetic

Author's note: Most of these poems take place in the years 1986-1989

# 1

*We believe too much in the singularity of our own terrible hearts*

## GIRL MONEY

The lifeguards at Park N' Pool
always got laid

with the girls who worked the concession stand.
The girls who worked the concession stand

poured vodka into the Slurpee machine
and stayed drunk for three months.

The lifeguards mostly broke up fights in the
kiddie pool and made sure teenagers didn't screw

in the five-feet but I could barely swim
and I looked stupid wearing a whistle.

When I asked about shoveling
with the landscaping crew

the college drop-out in charge
blew dope smoke in my face and said "Seriously?"

so I drove to the gas station
and pumped two gallons into the tank

of my parents' Oldsmobile Cutlass
twelve years old but still running.

The unemployment lines ran
from Pittsburgh east to Johnstown

and I wanted to buy beer
or maybe a gold necklace for my girlfriend

which is where I was headed
so we could fool around in her basement.

Her mom stomped around upstairs
cooking dinner, pasta again

but the sex was still lovely
still like taking flight

even when I climbed off
and she wiped her belly with a sock.

I wanted to bring flowers, roses
and not the short-stemmed kind

or take her to a movie
and not some two-dollar matinee

or buy her dinner at Houlihan's
somewhere nice that had appetizers

because girls were leaving boys
who didn't have money

boys who didn't show up
with wine coolers and teddy bears.

I drove west to Youngwood, past the jail
to New Stanton where my dad worked

in an auto plant on the assembly line
in the paint department, blowing sealant

with an air gun
even though he was an electrician

because they didn't need electricians—
they didn't need anyone anywhere.

Old men laid off from factories and ex-housewives
flipped burgers at McDonald's

and dropped the fries at Arby's and Rax
so I tried the golf course in Greensburg

but they weren't hiring
unless your parents were members.

My parents weren't members—
they believed in making money, not spending.

I knew one member
Mr. Connors

but he was a fucking creep —
he'd asked to see my dick

when I was twelve
and I still regretted not killing him

and anyway all he talked about was Harvard.
"Back when Harvard meant something" he said

and I thought: meant what, you pedophile?
I didn't need a recommendation to Harvard.

I didn't know what the fuck Harvard was
or what a martini was or where the door was

in that fucking goof's house on the hill
and I wasn't that desperate, not ever

so I drove to the Italian restaurant in Jeanette
where every customer was rumored

to be in the mob, know the mob
or owe the mob a million bucks

a left knee, a first-born daughter.
The guy outside parking cars said "Nah"

and inside the owner sat drunk at the bar
dressed in a bad sweater and a gold chain.

He handed me twenty dollars
and said "Seriously don't tell my wife."

Twenty dollars was a lot of money:
I had visions of perfume and silver earrings.

Down the road I pumped two more gallons of gas.
The gas station used to pump it for you.

At the country club I stood by the courts
and watched horny housewives rush the net

so their panties showed.
I would have taken minimum wage.

I would have taken less under the table.
The summer is an inferno when you're broke.

I would have been a disc jockey at the punk club
where all the pinheads slammed to Half-Life.

I would have carried kegs at the beer distributor
until the silver metal blimps broke my back in two.

I pumped another gallon into the tank
and found a payphone and called my girl.

I said "You don't know how much I love you."
She said "Let's go out tonight, let's play mini-golf!"

Mini-golf was six bucks with a coupon
plus drinks and snacks and more gas in the car.

I would have worked at The Hotel
running numbers and sweeping up peanut shells.

I would have emptied out the video poker machines
not swiped any quarters, made the night deposit

and rushed back to clean up
the all-you-care-to-eat taco bar.

I hoped to never work at the hospital
and I hated the nursing home

where the old people lined up
on the front porch in their wheelchairs

like racecar drivers going nowhere
but I tried to apply anyway

even after the receptionist said
"You're much too young"

and handed me a lollipop
not the application I reached for.

I pumped another gallon of gas
and headed home

while my girl
and beautiful girls everywhere

waited.

## HIRING ON AT THE SLAUGHTERHOUSE

Chris said "Do you want a job?"

and I said "Yeah"

       and the next morning

I saw a man take a knife to a squealing pig's throat.

## KILLING FLOOR

Dead cows the size of small cars
      and pigs so fat
      you could crawl
      inside their carcasses

      hung from steel chains
          dripping from the rafters.

If I could have walked on the ceiling
      I would have looked up
      and seen terrible balloons.

## THE MAN WITH THE LONG SILVER BLADE

called from his steel table
and I could smell the whiskey
from three feet away.

He was a meat cutter
    40 years old
    and made his living, as he once said
"carving real big roasts into real little roasts."

He stood at the top of the food chain
in the slaughterhouse, an okay guy
though once he threw a cow ball
at my head as a joke then pointed
his knife in a vicious stabbing motion
when I whipped the slimy testicle back.

Now he said "My wife is leaving me
and my daughter is fucking a drug addict.
    What about you?"

    and I said "I don't know."

    In the next room
the gears of the sausage machine ground gristle.
    It was an awful machine
equal parts mixing bowl and conveyor belt
    a tube shooting ground meat into pig guts
        literally guts

      meaning the cleaned-out intestines
      of the freshly killed sows.
Everywhere smelled of red peppers and vomit
      fennel and black pepper
      dried blood and bleach.
The intestines filled like skinny balloons
stretched over the nozzle of a helium tank.
      Squirt, fill, tie the intestine.
      Squirt, fill, tie, down the line.

I'd worked five hours without a break
and another five hours waited after lunch.

The man with the long silver blade
      rocked back and said
"What about you? You a drug addict?"

I'd seen adults drunk before, even swaying
in their boots, but not before lunch time
so when he asked "You want to score some blow?"

      I said "I don't know"
because desperation was not always truth.
Desperation was not even desperation
unless it was about money or love or both
      but not drugs, I thought, unless
      drugs were money or love.

I stayed in the room and shrugged.

He described the baggie out in his truck.
It sounded huge, though a grain of cocaine
sounds huge if you've never done cocaine
      and for years I thought
      an 8-Ball of coke was an 8-Ball
      until I bought an 8-Ball
      and it was the size of a ping pong ball
      and I told the dealer
      "Dude, you're ripping me off"
but that's later — now I said "I'll see."

      "You'll see is right"
the man with the long silver blade said
and did that stab with his knife again.

I wanted that cocaine and I didn't
      because
1) it exploded hearts
2) it exploded heads

      but
3) it did look fun in movies
4) guys in rock bands loved it

      And, anyways, I'd been
      a.)    smoking pot
      b.)    huffing glue
      c.)    huffing gasoline

    d.)    huffing paint thinner
             out in my parents' one-car garage.

In the breakroom, the owner laid out
a tray of lunchmeat and cheese.

Later, the meat cutter stumbled in.
He wore a little white butcher hat
and a blood-stained apron.
He looked like a praying mantis
        bug-eyed and small-handed
stuffing ham wrapped in bologna
into his mouth until he couldn't chew.

He mumbled "Come here."

I followed him to the stairs

and he said "I was just joking about that drug stuff"
and told me not to mention it to anyone else, ever.

So I didn't and I haven't until now

        but his eyes were the size of buzzsaw blades
        and his nose looked powdered with a knife.

We stood there and he put his hand on my shoulder
and I smelled the dead cigarettes on his fingers.

Then, without push or provocation, he fell back
    and stayed, bracing against
        the cinderblock wall.

## HOSING THE KILLING FLOOR

The hose struggled like a giant snake in my arms
and the animal fat melted under the hot water

as the blood turned to puddles
       then streams
              then rivers

except for the eyeballs, a dozen or so
which collected over the grate
       not knowing which way to stare
       rolling this way and that, looking lost

until someone came along
       and found them with his boot.

## MY BIG BROTHER WITH A BABY FACE

and no body hair except for one long strand
protruding from his left nipple like a wire
      parked on the side of the beer store.
He pointed at me in the backseat
      and said "Get out."

I got out, even though
I thought we were going
to Blue Dell Pool
      a mile down Route 30
to swim and talk to girls.

"You look 40" he said
and demanded my shirt

so I handed it over.

He pushed 12 bucks into my hand
      and said "Two cases of Piels."

I said "I have on Jams"
      Jams
    these flowered shorts
    popular with junior high kids.

    My brother said
"There's no dress code for being 21."

Both his goony friends nodded.
   One played JV hockey.
   The other bagged groceries
   at Foodland.
They would have happily punched
my balls until I folded over.

In the beer store
   clutching the crumpled bills
   trying to remember Piels
     two cases of Piels
I said — nothing, not even a stutter.

The guy behind the register said
"Get the fuck out" and laughed.

Back in the car, we headed east
and ended up on Tilbrook Road
   a couple miles from home.

My brother said "Get out"

so I did, again.

The car door slammed, the wheels turned
   and the three dry teenagers
drove into the rest of their summer without me.

I guess they found someone else to buy their beer.
I guess I was happy to be out of the car
        even though I was still shirtless
still in flowered shorts.

I started home in the July heat, dreaming.

If you are serious enough about your desires
they will appear, not like magic, but by practice
        by work, imitation, and devotion
even if your desires are not yet your desires.

The next time I came back
to that beer distributor
        a couple years later
        still under-aged
I had on coveralls
from the slaughterhouse
        dried blood under my nails
        and shit-kicking boots on my feet.

The same guy
        probably the owner
took a bite of a pretzel rod

and said "Yeah, what'll it be?"

**DOWN ON THE FARM**

The sun puts shadows
we barely understand

across the green grass

as the animals
walk from the fields —

death by hammer.

## JACKSON POLLOCK COULD HAVE SAVED OUR LIVES

The salt bed was a graveyard of cowhides
      a room-sized box
      of rotten wood
      and cracked concrete
filled with billions and billions of grains
      of coarse ground salt
           the extra 50-pound bags
           lining the walls
           like an army
           of penguins.

We buried the skins
until the leather company
wanted to buy the skins
then we dug up the skins.

There is the world, of course
then there is the representation of the world.

      Years later,
in a museum in Washington, D.C.,
      I stood in front
      of a Jackson Pollock painting
contemplating what it meant to be
      an abstract expressionist
      and/or
      a drip painter.

I imagined the slaughterhouse and the salt bed
>	but it was barely there
>	not nearly as powerful
>	as it would have been
if Pollock had dripped his paint into shapes
resembling the wood and concrete and skins
>	or the men who lost knuckles to saw blades
>	or the bottles they drank
>	to cope with the blood
>	or the dead cows that hung
>	like leather balloons from the ceiling.

But why do the difficult work of looking out
>	when it's so easy to turn in?

We believe too much in the singularity
>	of our own terrible hearts.

Because I am a sucker for things
I do not understand
>	I read a biography of Jackson Pollock
>	then saw the film about Jackson Pollock.
>	  Neither helped.

>	Pollock had a shrink.
The shrink encouraged Pollock to paint his pain
>	just the feeling, not the narrative.

Pollock would have been a better painter
if he would have painted his father, a farmer
        or the years he worked for the WPA
        or the bar where he crushed his liver.

There is the world, of course
then there is the representation of the world.

The representations I like best
are the representations that still resemble
people in crisis and the places they go
to save and/or destroy themselves.

Jackson Pollock is universally acknowledged
        as a genius.

You know that.

Forgive me for disagreeing.

You can't piss on canvas and call it art.

## BAR DREAMS

A man who drank Bud drafts at the Irwin Hotel
       said
in all sad seriousness

    "Kid, I ought to buy me a bar"

then mooched a dollar bill from my pile.

## WORLD AT WAR

*Anything can happen in the murk of the tavern*
-Cesare Pavese

I was underaged and the bartender was a veteran
of Korea who served me every third beer
on the house because I tipped well at closing time.

Most of the customers were laid off
from Volkswagen or Westinghouse.

Across the street at McIntyre's Pub
customers were throwing chairs again.
I'd seen a fight there the month before:
a small guy punched a big guy in the face
until the big guy's nose turned to mush.

Next door at The Lamp, poor families crammed
inside the theater to see a second-run flick.
The mothers, kids, fathers: all out of work.
Duct tape patched the tears in the red vinyl seats
and yellow stuffing still puffed out from the frames
> but a large bucket of popcorn was cheap
> and a small soda from the machine
> was a quarter.

The cop cruising Main Street got born again
but still carried his gun

        except when he taught Sunday school
        except in the hospital bed, dying of cancer.

The other cops brought flowers
and worked part-time
and took classes
at the community college.

I thought I knew everything about this town
        even the lives of people I would never know.

A shot of Jack Daniels was a dollar.
A Stroh's draft was thirty-five cents.

I had money from the slaughterhouse —
        all under the table, all tax free.

You want sad? I was the richest guy in the bar.

In the far corner, near the out-of-order jukebox
a man threw darts with the conviction of a soldier.

Later, a woman got yanked by her hair
from the bar by her husband and everyone froze.

Sitting on my red vinyl stool, I started
to wonder if the whole world was at war.

Outside: two voices, a car door, one voice
        the crank of an engine, gone.

The woman came back
	with fingerprints on her face.
She drank three consecutive shots and said
"What do you want to be
	when you grow up, little boy?"

I'd never beaten a woman before
	or been yanked from the bar
	by the roots of my hair
so I stood up and paid and wobbled to the door.

	Goodnight, gentlemen.

I started my car and backed into the movie theater
but it barely scratched my bumper.

	A cop showed with a flash of light and said
		"Are you drunk?"

	and I said "I don't know"

so he nodded and I drove off
	more sharp, less blind.

		Once
when I'd first started drinking at the Hotel
	a biker stood and announced
	that the problem
	with these new drinking-and-driving laws

>    is that they don't address how
>    you're supposed to get home from the bar.
>    Then he promptly passed out on the floor.

This all happened in 1988 and I remember it
more vividly than any Christmas or birthday
more vividly than any funeral or school dance
>    because I was blood
>    and when I grew up
>    I grew up
>    to be unemployed.

# 2

*Being young is a miracle:*
*You spend all day*
*in the dirt*
*with a shovel*
*and the world*
*refuses your grave.*

## THE FAKE ID

The picture on the driver's license is of my brother
      but the name is Douglas Olaf
      and his address is Toronto

and the old man behind the wooden bar
      at the bowling alley
      where no one ever bowls anymore
has a face like a leather boot.

The light in here is enough to make you squint
      and the lies I tell
      look better
      behind pulled curtains.

The old man checks the ID
      then checks my face.

"Twenty-four is pretty old" he says.

      I am in a white shirt
covered in brown blood and stink
and I have not shaved for three days.

He hands me the ID and says "One sixer of Bud?"

and I say "Better make it two"

which is taking advantage
of an obviously delicate situation
but at least I don't order a draft
and regale him with my bullshit
about 12 hours at the slaughterhouse
and a young family to feed.

He drops the six-packs into a brown paper bag
and says "You need any cigarettes?"

and I say "I don't smoke"

and he says "You should."

## SMASH IT UP

Friday night I banged the register
at the paint store for minimum wage

then woke Saturday morning
to pull hides at the slaughterhouse
for less than minimum wage
        but under the table.

It was summer and I hated work
but all my scams lacked distance
        and had gone kaput:
        no more fake joints to sell
            no more fake pills to deal.
Even the muscleheads
knew my steroids were bogus.

In the parking lot of the slaughterhouse
a guy on a motorcycle said "I ain't been home yet"
and swigged from a bottle of Early Times whiskey.
        He said "Want some?"

        and I said "Sure"

because I had been home
with my mother who loved God
        my mother who believed
            Heaven was a door

>     we knocked on
>     with our actions
>     and my actions
>     appeared despicable lately —
>         I puked loudly
>         and without illness
>         in the bathroom
>         behind a locked door
>         at odd hours
>     how I wrecked cars
>     how I fought strangers
>     how I came home late
>         or not at all.

At home my father was miserable
>     from the factory
>     from rumors of shutdown
>     of lock-outs
>     of closing for good.

I looked at these two people
>     one with a NIV Bible
>         the other with a monkey wrench
>         and some wire strippers
and I would have rather been drunk.

>     Terrance
one of the managers
>     said "Don't give a kid whiskey"

but the biker handed me the bottle

and I swigged and burned
    worried I'd puke
    but didn't.

The biker said "Nice work."
Terrance said "Stupid shits, both of you."

The whiskey barely hit
but still felt like possibility.

In the basement of the slaughterhouse
I pulled hides with a bunch of teenagers
    all guys, all friends
    the greatest guys and friends
    I thought I'd ever have
and the plans we made sounded like space travel:

    one kid would fly to the liquor store
    with his neighbor, the desperate cokehead

    another kid would moonwalk some weed
        from a creepy middle-aged
        baseball card collector
            and
    because I looked like I worked construction
        I would circle the distributors
        for one that served minors
        and buy the beer.

All night we slugged Old Milwaukee pounders
      inside a Mercury Cougar
      and raced backroads to avoid the cops
          and stopped occasionally
            to smoke dope and piss.

We fired empty cans off stop signs
and believed naked girls
      naked women even
were everywhere, waiting to bang us

but the girls and women never materialized

so we parked at McDonald's and gorged
on french fries and burgers, shakes and apple pies.
Teenage boys can eat a lot of junk
when they've hammered beers and dope
      and hoped to get pussy
and instead have driven miles
of green hills and wrong turns.

I ate a fry and went outside to the payphone.

I had the number of a woman
      who was 43
and willing to blow teenagers.
I thought I might surprise everyone
      with this brilliant news
because this woman had blown me before

>             but I'd shown up a second time
>             and she'd said "Dude, not kosher."
> She was very drunk and hanging
> with a guy who looked like a mechanic
>             a guy with large dirty hands
>             a greasy baseball hat
>             giant steel-toed boots parked by the door
>             and she kept me on the front porch
>                     saying nonsense
>             like "Honey, I didn't order a pizza"
> then finally whispered "You have to call first."

Now I dropped a couple quarters
        in a payphone
        but she didn't answer.
        I was very drunk
and hateful towards men who worked on cars.

All my pals stepped outside.

        I put down the phone
like I was putting away my dick
        at the end of a date
        with a girl who wanted to wait.

Next door was a Mister Donut
        so we moved there.

I guess we were going to smoke dope
or maybe dig out some more warm beers.

The Mister Donut looked condemned:
  dirty bricks, boarded-up windows
    dead shrubs, a crumbling parking lot.

I don't why I loved vandalism so much
or why some nights I controlled my body
and other nights my body controlled me

  but I knew I could put my fist
  through the back window
    thick as it was
    with wire laced through the glass

so I took a step and threw a hard right.

I'd thrown better punches
  but not at thicker windows.

The glass spider-webbed
  and my fist felt shattered
like a chain-reaction happened upon impact
  like my bones started to crumble
    first my fingers
    then my wrist
    on up to my elbow.

You can get off on pain
      especially if you're 17
      especially if you've run down on pleasure

and what's not to love
about bringing destruction
to a world that loves destruction—
      certain powers are accessible to us all:
if you cannot build it, knock it down.

Then I felt really fucking stupid

and Plumpy yelled "Let's go! Let's go!"

We loaded into the Cougar
      six guys jumping over each other.

Plumpy yelled "The cops are coming!"
and slammed the gas and pulled the stick
      into drive simultaneously
      and skidded and swerved
      60 mph down an alley
      between a KFC and a car wash
         more reckless
      than punching out windows
but we made the highway
then Route 136
then Beaver Road

         a road possibly named
         after a giant 1970s porn bush
despite the beavers and the dams
         down by the creek
         but that joke was so old
                  no one told it anymore
         and everyone finally calmed down.

Under the dome light
I checked my hand.
It looked swollen and slightly disfigured
         the knuckles cut red
         and glass in the cuts.

Plumpy said "Don't bleed on my car"

and I said "It's your mom's boyfriend's car"
but it was still nice enough not to bleed in.

I walked off in the woods to piss
but my fingers struggled
with the zipper on my jeans
until I finally switched to lefty.

A little sliver of moon shone down
         over the trees.

I could not imagine God
         or if I could
I did not want to anymore.

Plumpy dropped me off at midnight.

I tucked my fist in my pocket
    but my mom slept
    with the TV playing
    and my dad stayed
    at the factory
    for the overtime.

The next morning we attended church
    and I was very hungover
    like someone slammed my insides
    with a sledge hammer.
From the wrist down, I looked
like a monster, my deformed hand
growing lopsided or inflated with poison
    but this was another thing to ignore
    if we were to be holy and respected.

My dad wore a gray suit
and barely talked
but sang the hymns loudly.

My mom said the Lord's Prayer
with her eyes closed
    and pulled my arm hair
    when I dozed off—
    it was the same old shit
    and I felt like punching windows

       or smoking dope
       or drinking beer

or pulling hides at the slaughterhouse
            because
       even though the slaughterhouse
       promoted death
           and sometimes terror
       there was also whiskey

and the chance to speak in my own tongue.

## THE FIRST HANGOVERS
## ARE THE WORST HANGOVERS

Two hours into the shift
      our young heads
           black clouds
           raining down
           malt liquor and vodka

      my nose stuffed up
      from snorting something
      that someone later said
           was not drugs

one of the little guys
      said "I'm going to pass out"

and the fat kid in the corner
      said "I think I just shit my pants."

## DO YOU EAT MEAT?

An old man worked at a cow with a chainsaw.
    The blade tore the flesh
    and the sound was like a radio
    cranked up to 10 on a planet
    without any radio stations.
    He smiled but it did not mean
    what a smile was supposed to mean
        because he wore a t-shirt
        that read Killing Machine
        and he owned another t-shirt
        that read Dancing Machine
        and he had a necklace
        with gold-plated letters
        that read Fucking Machine
        but mostly he was a killing machine
        and he loved his job
        and he hated teenagers
            hated intrusions
            hated people
            who hated blood
            and death

and I was the teenage intruder
in the slaughterhouse of his life.

The old man waved like a puppet
    the way the sick
        purposefully show us sickness

and his goggles were splattered with muck
and still I could see his eyebrows bobbing.

Hello Fear and Hello Terror and Hello God
     I sometimes say
       to that distant world of my youth
thank you for teaching me about love.

The old man raised the chainsaw
and revved it three times
like a motorcycle about to lay tire
then sliced a six-foot cow down the middle
so one side of beef swayed on one chain
and another side of beef swayed on another.

He finished, conked out the saw, lifted his goggles
     and said "Do you eat meat?"

and I said "I do, I eat meat"

and I would have ripped a rib
from his body with my teeth
just to show I wasn't afraid

and still I would have been afraid.

He said "Well, you won't tonight"
and started the chainsaw again, dramatically

      but this is America
      where everyone eats meat
      no matter how it's killed
      no matter how it's broken down

because the table is the only place
that the world can never take
because Neruda once called roasted meat
      "the black boat of our dreams"
      before he shared his feast

      and
my mom who hated to cook
      had me light the grill
      and my dad
who usually worked through dinner
      flipped the burgers
      until they were pink
            but not bloody
      and we did not talk
      but filled our mouths
            each person nodding happily
            at the next person

      and later
I parked on Tilbrook Road
      with my girlfriend
      and we made love in the backseat
            twice

because she wanted to, because she let me
    then we disappeared into a diner
where we had breakfast at midnight
    eggs and bacon, eggs and sausage
    eating from each other's plates
        our hearts steady between us
    as hearts that share meals should be

and tomorrow, nearly 25 years later
I am going with my friend Neal
    to eat barbecue
    at a restaurant in Homewood
where a guy in an apron smokes meat
    on the sidewalk
and the sign in the window says:

    Stop Shooting
    We Love You

and it's true, every day, now,
    always

as the sky fills with smoke.

## PIG
*-for Neal*

Pig, I write this poem to honor you.
Pig, you are a hard animal to honor.
You are not like the pigs in the movies.
You do not learn tricks or inspire
spiders to write perfect words.
You have a brain the size of an egg
and you weigh three-hundred pounds.
Your nose is a shovel and a bulldozer
and you smash your face into mud with glee.
Pig, you are so fucking stupid.
Once you were a noble animal called a boar
and your tusks were sharp enough
to slice a hunter's leg down to the bone.
You ran wild in Africa and Asia
and instilled great fear in the natives.
Then you let yourself be caught and tamed
and bred with other pigs and now you are happy
to eat apple cores and dried corn.
You do not look up from the trough
when we kill your family for you are a pig
and selfish and completely uncaring.
You do not even bother to chew your cud.
Pig, you are not kosher.
Pig, the Qur'an calls you dirty.
Jews hate you and Muslims hate you.
Pig, you unite the world.

Only you can bring peace to the Middle East
where no one will eat you
and you will be condemned by all.
Pig, here is your poem.
Grow as large as America in America
where you will be eaten by all religions
and all ethnicities and all races.
Pig, stay stupid and fat and hated.

Thank you for tasting so delicious.

## THE WORST WEED I EVER BOUGHT

smelled great
didn't get me stoned
and tasted delicious
in a nice tomato sauce
over angel hair pasta.

## PLUMPY THREW UP

in the parking lot of the slaughterhouse
        then in the dressing room
                in a hamper
                filled with dirty uniforms.

He puked again on the concrete killing floor
        bent at the waist
                hands on his knees
and said "Shitfuck."

Each time a small volcano of yellow liquid
exploded in strings from his cracked lips.

"You going to be okay?" I said.

"No" he said and wretched.

He was still half-drunk
though he'd promised himself
he wouldn't drink before the match.

It was Saturday morning and he was 193 pounds.

At weigh-in on Tuesday night, he needed to be 167.

"Why not wrestle 185?" I said.

"Those bastards are strong" he said.

"You're strong" I said.

>Plumpy was a bear-hugging motherfucker.

He said "Not that strong."

Those bastards at 185 were coming down from 220.
> They ate broiled chicken
> and hamburgers they chewed
> and spit into napkins
> without swallowing
> and did push-ups
> by the thousands.

Plumpy said "Shitfuck, hell."

Everyone else on the team dressed in garbage bags
and ran bleachers until their hamstrings cramped
or stayed home and watched *Vision Quest*
> while drinking lemon juice
> through an eyedropper.

But Friday night
> Plumpy drank Old Milwaukee pounders
>> and smoked some dope
>> and tried to get laid
>> because, he said, beer was a diuretic

      and marijuana was fat-free
      and getting laid was exercise

    and anyway
he'd cut classes all week
to run laps around the gymnasium
in a plastic suit and ski hat.
Twice he'd bolted from Chemistry
to the lav because the laxatives
kicked in at the wrong time.

You can only destroy your health so much
      at 16 and a half
with exercise and diet
before better forms of destruction call.

But the beer and the dope and the not getting laid
      morphed his brain into an eating machine
          into a tapeworm of desire
          so we hit McDonald's
          and Plumpy ate
          two cheeseburgers and a large fries
          and drank a strawberry milkshake
          and a Coke the size of his head
with intentions to puke everything back up
      but it all tasted so good
      and his throat was raw anyway
so he ordered another round
      and another.

"Look" someone said "he doesn't just eat
         the cheeseburger
he makes love to the cheeseburger."

Plumpy stood up and wobbled.

He went home
         passed out
and forgot to throw up.

         Now
at the slaughterhouse
Plumpy stuck his fingers
down his throat
but nothing came up
except strings
of bile and snot.

         Down in the basement
Plumpy was my partner on the hide pull.

He was fucking useless
         sleeping on the salt bags
                  resting in the bathroom
gagging like a billy goat eating tin cans.

Then Plumpy disappeared.

On Tuesday afternoon
he showed up for Chemistry
with a garbage bag
under his sweatshirt
and slept face down on his desk
    so his cheeks drooped
    like melted wax
    and the sweat
    marched off his forehead
    like a clear liquid army.

I walked him to 5th period
    so he didn't drop in the hall

    but Tuesday night
in the locker room
    butt naked
he stepped on the scale
    at 167 pounds
    down to the ounce.

"Fucking told you" Plumpy said.

Being young is a miracle:
    you spend all day
    in the dirt
    with a shovel
    and the world
    refuses your grave.

    Shortly after this
Plumpy sprained his left knee
and permanently retired from sports

but not before a local sportswriter
    called him
    the new Mike Kirkland
        Mike Kirkland
        who was
        more or less
        the greatest name
        in the history
of Hempfield wrestling.

    That night
Plumpy ate an orange
and pinned his opponent
    in 39 seconds.

## THE COW WANTS HIS OWN POEM

and says so with his sloppy tongue.

>With his eyes
>he asks to be
>slaughtered
>more humanely

and with his stomach
he begs to eat grass instead of corn.

>Dressed
>in the black and white
>of the religious
>>the cow demands
>>to be worshiped

>>as a hamburger.

## THE HORRORIEST HORROR FLICK EVER

You see enough pigs thumped
in the snout with a hammer
and it all starts to look like death

    which, I guess, philosophically, it is

but death is barely death when you're a teenager.

It's not existential or even entertaining
    like in *The Big Sleep*
        one of my dad's favorite films
    when the broad says
"You're not very tall, are you?"
and the detective says "I try to be."

Guns in black-and-white films
made less sense than the guys
with guitars and big hair who
    I believed
spoke cultural wisdom.
I too wanted to fuck girls backstage
    even though I couldn't play or sing
    and I'd never been backstage
    because I couldn't afford concert tickets

so mostly I watched TV
    which

during the years 1986-1989
>	was MTV
>	the M standing for music
>	music defined loosely as fashion
> >	MTV
where fashionable guys with guitars and big hair
talked about getting laid with groupies
>	or guys with skinny ties and short hair
>	acted sad because they never got laid
or the occasional chick in spandex
clenched her fist and sang the songs
written by her egomaniacal husband
>	or Joan Jett in cheap high-tops
>	snarled and punched the air
> >	Joan Jett
>	who I just found out
> >	was a lesbian
>	when I said "Joan Jett is still hot"
>	and someone else said
>	"She's a lesbian"
>	which didn't make Joan any less hot
> >	or either of us any younger.

It was a very simple time, those years.
Everyone confused youth and wisdom.
>	Poor people who wanted money
> >	were greedy.
>	Rich people who wanted money
> >	were patriots.

The entire nation believed loud neon sweatshirts
mattered more than single mothers
    who couldn't feed their children.
A man crazy about an actress shot the President.
    The President had acted in nineteen films
        none of them watchable.
    When they dug the bullet
    from his lung, the President
    said God spared his life.
    Everyone loved God in the 1980s
    and God loved the President
    more than the President
        loved hungry children.

Jeff, my neighbor, subscribed to HBO
    which his mom
single and a waitress
    paid for in tips
    because she worked late
    and worried about
    Jeff being home alone.
I slept there a lot and sometimes
we drank cans of IC Light
and watched horror movies

    which brings me back to pigs
    getting hammered across the face:

I saw horror in the slaughterhouse:
    grown men with knives and saws
    lopping off various parts
    of various animals

and one guy asked
"You ever eat cow cock?"
    and
    laughing, laughing
    tossed a bloody dick
    like some horrible space worm
    through the air so it landed
    at my feet and shriveled.

I didn't need to see some fuckhead
in a hockey mask
whacking kids with a machete
    or another killer
    in a latex mask
    stabbing his sister
or Leatherface and his family of psychos
making meals out of visitors.

Every shift I worked I played the teenager
in the horroriest horror flick ever
so it didn't matter who had the chainsaw
    who got whacked or sliced or pureed.
Thinking was out. Action was in.
    The more terrible, the better.

The villains took up arms against us
        so we ran and they chased us
        through sequels and trilogies
                prequels and low-budget flops.

    They're chasing us now.

## THE CHAINSAW

The chainsaw takes down trees
so more grass can be planted, more hay.

The chainsaw takes down cows, splitting sides
so more people can be fed faster.

The world is filled with men and chainsaws.

Imagine a chainsaw with diamond teeth.

Imagine a chainsaw the size of a steak knife.

All praise the chainsaw.

This is all the chainsaw's fault.

## YOU CAN ONLY MISS 35 DAYS OF SCHOOL IN ONE YEAR AND STILL GRADUATE

Given the opportunity
    to stay in bed
    or attend a Physics class
taught by the Gym teacher
because the Physics teacher
    who had less seniority
    now taught Life Science
    to $7^{th}$ graders

I chose to stay in bed.

    On the day
of my $36^{th}$ absence

I started writing excuses
with a steady hand

    to duplicate
the nearly illegible script

    of a doctor
who I believed to be
    deceased.

## RAMBO, ROCKY, COW TAILS, BASTARDS

Did you have a little red wagon
when you were a kid? I did.
My first bike was metallic red
with a long black banana seat.

I knew a 40-year-old man
      who rode a bike to work
           who showed up exhausted
           and sweating like a pig.

You know what he did for a living?
    Cows.
    He took their skins
like a gentleman takes a woman's coat.

He had a long knife he loved.
He wore green fatigues.

What do you know about Vietnam?

As a teenager, I loved Rambo.
Rambo went to war, came home, went nuts.
    What could be cooler?

Maybe being a dumb Philadelphia boxer
who almost wins the World Title
against a dude twice as strong and fast.

Rocky broke legs for extra cash
        but he never liked it.
        I liked the pimp hat
                the leather jacket, too.
Do you remember that scene in *Rocky*
when he's using a meat cooler as a gym
        training in the cold
        whacking a side of beef
        like an Everlast punching bag?
                I did that.
I hung around beef hanging around a meat locker.

The guy who rode his bike to work?
Everybody said he'd been in Vietnam
        for two tours.

He liked to say "You pansy-ass punk"
which reads silly but he made it sound mean.

He once threatened to stab me for touching
the front tire on his bike, which looked flat.

While I hid in the basement of the slaughterhouse
        he worked upstairs by a window
        where he could see his bike
        chained outside to a green dumpster.

        The dead cows
        tied up with chains

       moved to him
       on an electric belt
       with the push of a button
            like shirts
            at the dry cleaners.

With his hunting knife and strong fingers
       he separated the outside of the cow
            from the inside
            then tossed the warm bloody skins
            down a metal chute
            to the basement
where I buried the skins in salt
       to make sure they stayed fresh
            until
            weeks later
when the leather company
showed up with a dump truck
       and I dug the skins up.

Do you remember your little red wagon
       how it had a nice handle you could pull?

Cows skins were like that—
you could grab their dead tails and yank—
       the salt would fall off
and the job was simple and easy.

Without a tail, I dug and pulled
 dug and pulled, a total bitch.

 Up on the killing floor
 past the slaughter line
the man who rode his bicycle to work
 who talked to his knife
 like it was his girlfriend
hacked off those precious tails
and tossed them in the trash.

The hate between us was strong enough
 to almost resemble love.

He trimmed those tails down to nubs, the bastard.

# 3

*What kind of shitty country are we living in that bowling is too expensive?*

## SCOTTY

Scotty whose dad owned a club
and drank Black Velvet whiskey

Scotty whose mom lived in a trailer
and smoked too many cigarettes

Scotty whose sister was hot
      and could fight
and worked evenings
at the grocery on Route 136

Scotty whose dad called him Rabbit
because he ran the 40 faster than the skinny kids
      the wide receivers and cornerbacks

Scotty who should have started at fullback
      but hated the coach
           a middle-aged nutjob
           who dated a 10$^{th}$ grade girl

Scotty who would have rather drank in a field
than played football anyway

Scotty with the beautiful girlfriend
      the beautiful girlfriend
         who had, everyone said, great tits

Scotty with the beautiful girlfriend
       he couldn't trust
who listened to Madonna
and talked about being a stripper.

Outside at the McDonald's
       Scotty waited for Eli Bausch
       who was rich
       who went to a private Catholic school
       who dressed in Bill Cosby sweaters
           and gelled his hair
Eli Bausch who may have been fucking
       Scotty's girlfriend
       the one with the best tits in school—

              we'd soon find out.

## SCOTTY'S DAD BOUGHT A BAR

or bought into a bar
or bought a liquor license
and used it to open a bar
with a guy who owned
      a cinderblock building.

Nights he served drinks
      washed the glasses
           cleaned the restrooms.

Days he worked in a factory
      servicing the assembly line
        until the bar turned a profit
then he quit being a millwright

and started drinking at the bar
he either bought or bought into

until the bar became someone else's bar

and his wife became someone else's wife

and his driver's license belonged
to the state of Pennsylvania.

For months he moped around the living room
      in his boxer shorts

       and attended AA meetings
       until the state returned
       his license
       and the factory
       took him back
       but without
       his seniority.

Weekends, he drank at the VFW
where a glass of beer was 50 cents
and the women were better than average

       while
as a last resort
his son and his son's pals
pilfered his liquor cabinet
for bottles of Johnny Walker Black

while dreaming our own dreams
       of alcohol and success.

## OWEN, THE OWNER OF THE BOWLING ALLEY, IS 91 YEARS OLD

and hates teenagers
      though teenagers
      are the only people
      who come to
      the bowling alley anymore.

What happened to all the leagues
      that used to fill the lanes
on Tuesday, Wednesday, and Thursday nights?

Those people
      in their ridiculous shirts
had money and bought drinks
and ordered pizzas from the bar.
It was an orgy of nimwits
screaming at standing pins
and praying to God
like God gave two shits
      about gutterballs.
What kind of fuckhead
takes his wife bowling
      for a date?
These guys did it for years
and the wives apparently liked it.
They drank like men
and puked in the stalls like men

and sometimes left their bloody tampons
.....on the floor, the bitches.
Then they quit liking bowling
and drinking beer until midnight.
.....Wives start stupid but end
.....smarter than their husbands.
They learn not to bowl
and start drinking white wine.

The bowling alley was crowded for years
.....then abandoned.

Owen offered a drink special
.....but it was too late.
No one thought a bottle of Esquire
.....for 75 cents was a big deal.

The diner across the street closed.
The pizza shop closed.
The factory did not close
but they talked about closing.

.....Years ago
Owen worked in a mine
then worked construction
then bought a restaurant
then bought this bowling alley.

You can't do that anymore in America.

It's all scraps now, hand-me-downs
from the rich fucks in three-piece suits.

Kids going to college was a fucking mistake.

We should have armed the women with shotguns
and lined them up outside the factories
        to protect the jobs.

Now all you can do is work at a box store
        and eat popcorn on your break
        and maybe steal some batteries at closing.

Owen saw one of the old jerks
        from the bowling league
        down at K-Mart
and said "What happened to you?"
and the guy said he lost his job
and couldn't afford to socialize anymore.

What kind of shitty country are we living in
that bowling is too expensive?

Owen hired three girls
        to work the all-night bowling
        on weekends.
The teenage girls
        think he is cute
        and they charm him

with their smiles and fat titties
that fall out of their tank-tops.

Owen's wife is dead for thirty-one years come June
and she never wore a tank-top
but sometimes cried during sex.

Owen hasn't had a hard-on since 1978
but the time for a comeback is now.
A dick is like a boxer — it just needs training
and the chance to make it big.

Owen sometimes dances with a broom
to make the new girls laugh.
These dumb bitches barely know who Elvis is
let alone Nat King Cole.
They do their homework and drink Cokes
they steal from the machine with keys
he should never have given them.

Owen sometimes sits in the parking lot
across the street
and watches the happenings
of his bowling alley
as run by three teenage girls
and the musclehead boys they admit
without charging.

What does it matter if they steal
or fuck in the storeroom?

What does it matter that they will grow up
      to be doctors and vote Republican
      or end up loading boxes off a truck
      for minimum wage
      or sucking dick in a strip club for tips?

The worst is that some days 91
      feels like a new beginning.
Owen knows everything there is to know
      but is too tired to do it.

      Outside in the alley
he smokes unfiltered Camel cigarettes
      because they taste delicious
      and are good for his health.

## OWEN, 91 YEARS OLD AND WORRIED, HEADS OUT

One of the teenage girls who worked at the bowling alley quit by not showing up.

The other two teenage girls said "She wants to be a stripper."

Owen said "No one wants to be a stripper."

The girls said "Duh, have you seen her tits? They're huge."

The girls talked like this, as one, a big gob of pink and bright yellow.

Owen said "The bowling alley is a fine job."

The girls said "We like it."

The strip club existed, but barely, out in Smithton, a hillbilly-hellhole town with a dirt-lap race track and a bottling plant owned by the woman who used to be on *The Partridge Family*. Owen liked that show. Not one of the actors could sing or play but they looked good, looked wholesome, even though the manager was a dick-knocker who only cared about money. Owen sometimes imagined himself as a showbiz manager, only with more smarts and class. He'd always wanted to meet Ray Charles and drive the negro club circuit and fuck with the cracker cops who tried to keep the afternoon shows segregated.

Owen said "How do you girls know about this strip club?"

They said "We know lots of things!" and giggled.

They said "How do you know about this strip club?"

Owen said "That is the million-dollar question."

He started the popcorn machine because melted butter helped him think.

Owen said "Does your little friend have a daddy?"

The girls said "He's an accountant."

"And he doesn't care his little girl is shaking it on stage in the buff?"

The girls shrugged. One girl put her necklace in her mouth and sucked. The other girl adjusted her bra.

Owen said "You ladies like popcorn?"

They said "It's more fattening than four quarter-pounders from McDonald's."

Owen said "That's a lie" and found the salt shaker in the cabinet.

The girls said "How do you stay so skinny?"

They said "You look good for being so old!"

All this conflicted Owen. He liked pussy as much as the next 91-year-old man and he believed the women's libbers were right about many things like jobs and being able to get on the pill. Owen often recollected being disappointed that he was too old to enjoy the free love of the 1960s but here it was 1988 and showing your tits and snapper at a one-dollar strip club where truckers beat off in the bathrooms was no way for a teenage girl to earn spending money.

Owen said "Take care of the popcorn, ladies. Make sure you spray all the shoes with disinfectant when the bowlers hand them back in."

They said "You can trust us!" and saluted.

No one was in the bowling alley. They all looked around. The video games sat unplugged in the next room.

Owen took a can of beer from the bar, one of the three he allowed himself each day, and drove west towards the Turnpike and Smithton. It was a boring drive and Owen imagined himself spanking the teenage girl's ass on stage until she asked to be driven home to her neglectful parents or submitted a written apology for not calling off at the bowling alley.

The strip club was worse than he remembered: a giant aluminum bucket with a gravel lot and a few shady parking spots for illegal commerce.

The bouncer looked black and Chinese, mixed, handsome but sort of feminine.

Owen said "You're not going to check my ID?"

The bouncer said "I guess I could" and smiled politely.

Inside, the girls grinded against poles and rocked on some ridiculous swing and generally made fools of themselves with their genitals out. The club didn't serve booze because it was illegal to show a full-naked twat and get drunk simultaneously in the great state of Pennsylvania.

Owen ordered a Coke and, imagining the soda was spiked, stirred it with his finger.

The teenage girl who used to work at the bowling alley saw Owen and waved.

The other teenage girls were right: this one had big cans. Tits that big embarrassed Owen.

The girl said "Hey Mr. Owen!" and danced over to him.

He said "What are you doing here?"

She said "Auditioning."

He said "Your daddy is an accountant."

She said "Act like you think I'm sexy. It will make the owner hire me."

None of this made sense to Owen and yet it did. He put twenty dollars in the girl's panty-bottoms and gave her a gentle pat on the ass. If his dick still worked, or if he was interested in working his dick, it would have sprung to life.

The girl said "Twenty dollars is too much" and blushed.

Owen said "You deserve it."

She said "This is more work than I imagined."

Owen said "I bet" and noticed sweat beading behind the girl's fine black mustache.

She said "Mr. Owen, you're the best" and undid her bra and moved on to the next guy, a fat man with a page-boy haircut and a knit glove with the fingers cut off on his right hand.

Owen threw two more fives and a couple ones to the middle of the stage where the other creeps couldn't steal it and stood up.

He wondered if he'd ever been a creep.

Being a creep was not so hard to do.

Outside, in the car, in the shade, Owen started the air conditioning and decided to sleep. A little warm beer sloshed around the bottom of the can but Owen felt too tired to drink.

## OWEN VOTES FOR WALTER MONDALE

Since Ronald Reagan took office
this country has taken a serious shit-dive.

All that California bastard does is look handsome
and yak about family values

while his third wife smiles politely
and talks to astrologers

and his daughter spreads her pussy
for some skin magazine.

So what, Reagan talks tough to the Russians
about bombs and freedom —

Owen talks tough to the Russians
every night after his third beer:

hey Russia, go fuck yourself.
Drink another vodka, you commie pricks.

Owen remembers Herbert Fucking Hoover
that great American jackoff

who would have rather fed cows
than out-of-work Americans

because feeding poor Americans
would have lowered their dignity

or some such shit.
Owen's parents were in West Virginia

starving, not hungry, starving
until FDR got elected, thank God.

Fuck you, Herbert Hoover
Owen sometimes thinks still.

Hoover allowed people to live in tents
and eat rotten apples stolen from carts.

All these years later and the best
the underdogs can offer is Walter Mondale.

The factory jobs drift off to China
and Taiwan and all old Walter Mondale can do

is accuse Reagan of being a showman—
well, no shit, he acted in Hollywood.

Of course he's a showman, you are too Mondale
but a shitty one, a boring white guy in a bad tie

with bad hair and no nuts, afraid to call Reagan out
for crushing unions and attacking poor people

but come this election
Owen will be voting for Walter Mondale

same as the six or so other people in America
who haven't lost their fucking minds.

## WHAT BECAME OF CRAZY ED, THE WORLD'S GREATEST JUGGLER OF COW BALLS

A meat cutter dressed in bloody coveralls
asked if I'd seen old Ed around.

Another middle-aged psycho
leaned and smoked and said
    "You sure
      you ain't seen Ed around?"

    I nodded.
I definitely had not seen Ed around.

When I did see Ed around
    I avoided him
like I would have avoided these two guys
perched in the dressing room
    like crows on a telephone pole.

The meat cutter said "Fucking Ed."

The psycho said "Sick fucking bastard."

I said "You guys want to talk about Ed?"
    which sounds sort of bold
      but definitely was not.

One said no, the other shook his head
	then one said "Fucking Ed"
	and the other said "Goddamn right."

Because this is what they did, always
	talked until the facts were rumors
		and the rumors were facts:
nutty Ed, lovable Ed, Ed who was loco
	good old Ed probably a sped
	Ed who would do anything
	Ed who ate an eyeball on a dare
	Ed who ate raw meat from the grinder
	Ed who juggled cow testicles
	like a demented clown.

Had I seen old Ed the sped around?
Or had that dumb motherfucker
chucked the glamour of pig guts and retired?
Old Ed could be dead, hard to tell about a man
who spent 15 of his 26 years on this earth
	trying to suck his own dick.

	Outside
on his way to slaughter
	a cow said
in one desperate syllable:
	moo.

"That crazy old Ed" the meat cutter said again.

"Yup, what a goofy fucking bastard"
    the psycho said.

I said "I don't know" and shrugged
    one boot on
        lacing the other boot
        as fast and nonchalantly
            as I could

because I was Ed too
    anyone
    could be an Ed —
this was a place of shitstorms and setbacks
to help move the hours on the time clock

and the real Ed lurked in corners.

He had acne that oozed pus and bled
and everyone said he was retarded
though he sometimes spoke thoughtfully
    things like hello / goodbye / how are you
        the vowels drawn out
and once he handed me
a dandelion with a long green stem
    though another time
    he smashed a glass
    over his own head
    for laughs.
    For laughs

      he also ate a light bulb.
      He spit on things
      and at people
      and could snot-rocket his sinuses
           seemingly at will
      to clear out the blood-and-death stink
      of the slaughterhouse.

Forgive me for telling the truth about Ed:
he did not speak thoughtfully
      only slowly and sometimes coherently
      usually about violence
the football player he most wanted to kill
      (Bubby Brister)
or the boxer who most deserved to die
      (Mike Tyson)
or the woman he most wanted to fuck
      (Bo Derek).
The only music Ed listened to
was Black Sabbath
and he waved devil signs
when he sang the guitar riffs
and the lyrics about demons
      and metal monsters.
He claimed to have watched
*Rambo: First Blood Part II*
      more than 100 times.
He claimed to own a rocket launcher.

   The meat cutter said
"They caught Ed jerking off with hamburger."

   The psycho said
"Jerking off with hamburger, it's true."

I had my boots on and tied
   one foot pointed toward the door.

The windows muted the sun
with thick blocks of glass.

"Jerking off with hamburger?" I said.

"Supposed to be like fucking a ghost"
   the meat cutter said

and I was out the door
and down the stairs
   across the killing floor
   through the sausage room
   down another flight of stairs
     rotten wood this time
   into the basement
   where they kept the cow hides
     buried in salt
   and the smell of blood
   was as unavoidable as oxygen.

One of my pals said "You're late."

Another one said "You hear about Ed?"

and I said "That he got caught
jerking off with ground meat?"

and he said "No, that's disgusting"
      then went on to explain:

Ed had been fired
for fucking a 300-pound pig.

## A MIDDLE-AGED DRUG DEALER

who nicknamed himself Dribble
    who used to be a high school basketball star
wanted to be paid in baseball cards, not money

but my friend Shawn loved baseball
at least as much as getting stoned

    especially Roberto Clemente
    dead now 18 years
        who fell from the sky
        between Pittsburgh
        and Nicaragua
            delivering food
            to earthquake victims.

What an angel that guy was in right field
    locomotive on the bases
        a steel mill at the plate
            twice pounding 100 RBIs
            and 3000 hits overall.

Roberto Clemente
    who led the Pirates to two championships
Roberto Clemente
    who blasted a solo home run
    in game seven
    of the 1971 World Series

and all of Pittsburgh exploded with love —
    grown men with black lungs
    clutched their 200-pound wives
    while the transistor radios sang.

"Not my Roberto Clemente" Shawn said

    but Dribble
standing seven feet tall
with hands to palm a human head
    was insistent.

The life Shawn led was not the life
    Shawn wanted to lead.
Never had it been more clear than standing
in this shithole apartment in Youngwood
    holding what remained of his childhood
    in one hand, a cold Budweiser in the other.

    Roberto Clemente wouldn't have sold
        his Roberto Clemente
    Topps bubblegum baseball card
        to an ex-jock drug dealer
        unless it saved some kids
        in South America

and that kind of love and dedication
    was the kind of thing
    that made Shawn want to get stoned.

Bless you, Roberto Clemente.
    We all can't be you.

And Jesus, it was Friday
and the world was still the world
    and the Pirates hadn't won the Series
        in almost a decade.

When Dribble asked
    one more time
    for the 1971 Clemente card
    Shawn dropped it on the table
        baseball safe in his memory
        another major loss
        another minor victory
    his pocket filled with a bag
    of Alaskan Thunderfuck
rumored to be some very primo weed.

## HARRY HAD A BUNCH OF FOOD STAMPS

and wanted to sell them for half price
so we stood outside the Dandy Dollar
while rain pounded like BBs
      on the aluminum awning
      and Ernie
      the manager
bobbed his bald head
and eyed us through the glass.

Harry had two jobs and five kids.
      Sleeves of engine grease
      covered both his arms
      and his teeth
      looked like
someone had bowled a spare in his mouth.
      Harry's wife was dead
      and everyone said it was syphilis
      or maybe tampon disease
and now those kids were skinny as stray dogs.

My mom delivered food from the church
to their wooden house with a hole in the roof.
Harry accepted the food but politely declined
the invitations to attend Sunday services
while his kids wore dirty clothes and ran shoeless
across their gravel driveway into the mud.
      "Oh Harry"

      the church women said condescendingly
because Harry did not know how he had sinned.

      Now Harry said
"This is 38 dollars worth of food stamps
and all I'm asking is 20 bucks."
Harry looked at Ernie's bald head
      and maybe thought of my mom
      and those righteous ladies
      delivering casseroles
      and leaving their Bibles behind
and he said "No one has to know about this."

      But I knew about this.
I knew the Sermon on the Mount
      and the Sermon on the Plain.
I knew the Beatitudes—
blessed are the hungry
      for ye shall be filled.
I knew the Christians—the ugliness of sex
      the terribleness of alcohol
            the eternal flames of Hell
                  how the Rapture
                  would lift my parents
                  like angels into the sky
                  and leave me behind
                  with the Antichrist
                  and the sign of the beast
                  and horses riding

        through flames
        to strike me
and Harry and his children
        and everyone else
        down.

I hated the Christians so much
I wanted to be like Jesus:
    blessed are the poor
    the hated, the meek, the merciful.

Harry said "It's a good deal."

I knew people on food stamps
    the great secret, the great shame —
they shopped the grocery stores late
when the aisles were empty
and acted quickly at the cash register
while the rest of us in line looked away
like food stamps were a crippled leg
    an abomination from God.

Harry said "I won't tell your mom"
and smiled his yellow-toothed smile

while I went in my pocket for a 20.

Opportunity is opportunity
    and Harry sold it like a gift.

I took those food stamps everywhere
        rolling like an itinerant preacher
from the church of one beer store
to the gospel revival of the next

until the bartender at the Flagship Inn
finally said "You can't buy sixers of beer
with welfare checks, you dipshit"

        and so I bought nothing
        from nowhere

because the reality of charity is this:
        yellow cheese and cheap meat
            white bread and generic cereal.

When I saw Harry again
outside the Dandy Dollar
        I handed back his food stamps
            38 dollars worth
        and all the money in my pocket
        probably six or seven bucks
because once a man has exhausted
        all the possibilities
        for his own worldly success

it's easy to open the Gates of Heaven
        for another lost soul.

## TERRANCE TAKES HIS KIDS TO DAY CARE

Last year they lived with his mom
in her half-remodeled basement
>    two walls completed
>    no insulation
>    fireplace without fire
>    bathroom without a door.

Everything smelled like mold and detergent.
The two boys slept in one twin bed
bought used from a neighbor and missing screws.
Terrance slept on the floor in a sleeping bag.
The pipes pinged with air and woke Terrance
when he needed sleep —
>    two jobs and the community college:
>    days at Arby's as an assistant manager
>    weekends at the slaughterhouse
>>        telling white teenagers
>>        to clean the killing floor
>>        or stack the cow hides neatly
>    then evening classes in political science
>    to get back to a university
>>        then law school.

This year they have a three-room apartment
in Wilmerding
>    better than Pitcairn
>>        maybe worse than Turtle Creek.

These old mill towns all look the same:
no jobs, average schools, bars
that open at seven AM and cash welfare checks.

The older boy is 12 and made states
in wrestling but states costs money
        hotels and sign-up fees
        new wrestling shoes
        head gear, new singlet
                time off work
so they stayed home and went to McDonald's
for breakfast and ate those pancakes
that taste like puffed-up cardboard.

The kid said "But dad?"

and Terrance said "Eat your pancakes."

The younger kid has autism.
He's smart but weird
        reads the dictionary
                will hug but does not
                like to be hugged back.

Terrance's mom is an alcoholic.

Terrance's dad
        now deceased
                was an alcoholic.

Terrance's wife is in the women's prison
    for hitting a kid on a bicycle
—hitting, not killing, she'll remind you—
    when she was drunk.
Now she sends letters talking about God
but doesn't ever ask about her sons.

Now he has a safe place for his children.
They have their own room
and Terrance sleeps on the couch
    which is fine.
    He likes to be near the door
        to have the jump on whoever knocks
            even if it's God.

Fuck God, Terrance thinks.
God can stay in the letters delivered from prison.

Terrance has never had a drink.
Terrance has never done a drug.
He cleaned up his dad's puke
    and his mom's puke
        emptied the garbage can
        in the upstairs bathroom
        when it filled with empties of Schlitz
woke both parents for work
    and called work
when his parents would not wake.

Monday morning Terrance gets up
and takes the kids to daycare by himself.
    Tuesday he does it again.

## LONNIE IS RELEASED AFTER MORE THAN THREE YEARS ON THE INSIDE

Outside the prison
       in her own jeans and her own blouse
       breathing her own air, not the state's
she takes a bus downtown.
Outside the bus
       she walks to a payphone
       on Liberty near 5th Avenue
and drops her own quarters in the slot
and speaks in her own voice into the receiver.

       She did 1219 days
for hitting a kid on a bicycle.
She was drinking, yes, but not drunk
and the kid rolled in front of her.
       White kid on a bicycle
is how she says it in her mind
but that thought is useless now.

She has two hundred dollars
       mostly from working laundry.

She found God inside
but outside it all feels like God:
the bridge with the hundred-foot drop
       the stadium across the river

        even the hooker with a skirt so short
        you can see her ass cheeks.

Inside, there was a cell the size of a bed
    a sink, a shitter
and a woman resting above Lonnie
who said "God will make this right."

Maybe God made it right.

Maybe Lonnie made it right.

She has not thought about what she loves
since they stripped her down
and dressed her in an orange jumpsuit

but she is on the bridge now
    sky above
        water below

and out there, 18 miles away, are her two kids
who she has loved so much and so quietly
in her terrible heart
her heart that only pumps for her two children
      her two children
      who she refused to imagine
even when she was elbow-deep in hot laundry
    with nothing to think about.
      Prison is a terrible place

      and the thoughts you think
      can become terrible
      to the people you love
      if you think them
      so Lonnie never imagined
      her children or spoke their names.
      She only said and thought God
            but in her mind
            the mind beyond her mind
            God was her children
            and her children were God
            but not
            so the kids would not be tarnished
            in the outside world
      while Lonnie ate oatmeal in a paper bowl
      and a woman in the next cell
      got strip-searched by two lady guards
      who liked to throw elbows and punch.

One boy is supposed to be a wrestler
and the other has problems with his brain
but her husband says they are both capable of love
      and miss her very much.

The cab comes but Lonnie has wandered away
from where she was supposed to be picked up
and she has to run to not be left behind.

Monday she will get a job.

Monday night she will love her boys
and, if he will allow it, her husband.

Nothing she does in this world
will ever be for herself again.

# 4

*It's hard to imagine
but I learned to love language
by reading words I hated*

## A LINE OF POETRY

I'm not bragging but I was the best poet in Creative Composition circa 1988 at Hempfield High, a school named after the marijuana that grew wild on the hills and in the fields of Western Pennsylvania. The best poem I wrote that semester was an A-B-C-B rhymer called "Looking Bowl" and it was, all my classmates agreed, very deep.

Maybe I wasn't the best poet in Creative Composition but the other guys in the class either wrestled or played football. Guys writing poems really pissed the coaches off. I was done pissing coaches off and running laps until I puked on the sidelines. I was done with everything.

Why I didn't quit school I can't imagine except my dad would have backslapped my head into pulp, and auditorium study halls were still the best places to meet girls.

The girls in Creative Composition wrote poems about daisies, and the poems we read in the textbook were about daisies, and the poems the teacher read aloud were about daisies and lilacs and urns. An urn, the teacher explained, was similar to a vase, pronounced *vaaz*.

*Vaaz* — I want to kill myself, writing this, thinking of the hours I lost to nonsense. But I don't blame the teacher.

In 1988, you could get arrested for pretending students were intelligent enough to read a poem written about something other than a flower.

I didn't write about flowers, even when that was the assignment. I only skimmed the textbook to pass the quizzes and I sometimes slept during lectures but when called upon to read my work I read my work, something most of the boys refused to do, especially the dudes who hung around the art room and drew dragons blowing dope smoke.

Maybe I was stoned when I read my work aloud but it didn't help. My voice quivered over my own lines and my end rhymes made me flush red and sweat but having written made me proud because I did not look like a writer. I looked like a dumb lug with bad part-time jobs.

I did not know you could write about bad part-time jobs so I did not write about the man at the slaughterhouse standing over a pig with a sledge hammer. The teacher did not say the words *sledge hammer* even once that semester.

The teacher never said a nice word about my poems and I never said a nice word about her teaching but I stayed up late with a pen and a notebook writing more than I could ever turn in.

I wrote enough poems for what I imagined was a book.

Later that year I went to the library and borrowed a book of love poems called *The Passionate Pilgrim*. The only author I recognized was Shakespeare who I had misread and misunderstood many times in many English classes and had learned to hate. I read *The Passionate Pilgrim* a dozen times or more. It was awful. I knew it was awful. I couldn't get enough of the awfulness, an awfulness more awful than the Bible, which only ever made me think *thee* and *thou* and *whilst* and *doth*, instead of salvation or hell or King David or war or even prostitutes weeping.

It's hard to imagine but I learned to love language by reading words I hated. Every syllable of confusion and boredom slammed around my brain until I felt humiliated enough to move in the world and find poems written by the living and the recently deceased, poems where the men and women on the page moved like nurses and factory workers and musicians.

It took years to find a great book.

One of the great books said "My teachers could easily have ridden with Jesse James for all the time they stole from me."

Which brings us back to my poems, one starting with the line "I choke down my boiling illegal poison" which, I explained to my pal, meant "I drink a can of warm Old Milwaukee."

Everything I wrote needed to be explained because everything I read needed to be explained.

No one told me you could write directly and honestly and in detail, so every thought I had, every moment I experienced, I translated into something profoundly stupid and purple.

In "Looking Bowl," my masterpiece, a poem that started "Through my bowl this world I see / in peace and love and harmony," I disguised the art of getting stoned, I explained to my pal, and my pal nodded, and we passed the bowl, and I felt pretty good about everything and not like punching someone in the head.

Punching someone in the head—now that's a line of fucking poetry.

# 5

*The biker offered me another beer.*

*How do grown men
men with gray in their beards
end up working in a slaughterhouse
and living in aluminum boxes
and supporting kids they never see?*

*I took the beer.*

## HONOR ROLL FOR VANDALS

With scissors and the morning paper
Plumpy rushed into homeroom
and said "Look, you made it!"
then showed me the tidbit
from the *Tribune* police blotter
    five lines detailing
        the window I'd smashed
        at the donut shop.

In his biography of Pretty Boy Floyd
    Mark Waters wrote
about all those Depression-era bad guys:
    "They knew the only way to fame
        was crime."
    Maybe we all know that:
    talent can't match corruption.

"You should be proud" Plumpy said
    and cut out the article
    a two-inch square
    of newsprint
and taped it to my locker

just like my mom used to do
    on the refrigerator
    with my accomplishments
    back in 9th grade
the last year I made the Honor Roll.

## MARGARET CALLED GOD AND GOD WASN'T THERE

Dear Mr. Death—

I hope to kill a couple guys in bars
so other guys in bars buy me drinks
and their women all blow me.
Let me die while being blown, Mr. Death.
Let me die while fucking in a cemetery.
Is this asking for too much?
I'll be 18 in three months and I feel old.
The creepy guy at the gas station
says I have a porn-star mustache.
Is it wrong to hatchet his fat skull?
There are many fat skulls to hatchet.
I should hatchet my own fat skull.
I've seen it in the movies and on TV.
Maybe telling myself I want to die
is the best way to keep from dying.
Maybe 100 years will come and not be enough.
Save me from the tree and the car.
Save me from the alcoholic overdose.
Save me from the sensible miracles
my mother and father pray for me.
I don't even need to kill those guys in bars.
I don't even need to win the fucking fight.
I can take a punch and don't mind unconsciousness.
At 17, victory is a beautiful middle-aged woman

with a tattoo on her tit, nursing my busted nose
with an ice-filled rag and kisses on my forehead.

Are you there Death?

It's me, Dave.

**THE DETAILS**

A boy threw a piece of bologna
      straight up

so the bologna spun
like a flying saucer

while a man
in rubber boots
so he could muck
through the blood
on the killing floor
      cleaned his teeth
      with a knife.

Never understand
what you don't need
to understand.

Understand everything.

## A CONCISE LESSON ON THE DELICACIES OF CUISINE IN FOREIGN COUNTRIES AND HERE AT HOME BY TWO LIFETIME SLAUGHTERHOUSE EMPLOYEES

Because they threw pig eyes like ping pong balls

Because they pelted us with bull balls
    because the testicles
      were slimy and hard as rocks

Because I ran
    and slid on a puddle of blood

Because a man older than my father
stuffed a testicle down the back of my shirt

Because there are lessons to be learned:
    bull balls, they said, were a delicacy
    in many foreign countries
    and chefs for kings
    called them Mountain Oysters

and the butcher wearing a funny hat
    smoking a Marlboro Red
    said "Foreign countries like Kentucky"

    then asked me if I'd ever eaten any ass.

## MEDICAL SCHOOL WAS PROBABLY OUT

of the question, I thought, as I choked down
       a can of Old Milwaukee
because a biker with dice tattooed on his neck
said canned beer made the best medicine
       for a hangover.

       For the last few months
my mom had been saying
       "You should go to medical school"

       but a year before
admiring one of my terrible report cards
she'd said "I don't care about your grades.
Your relationship with God is more important."

My relationship with God was nonexistent
       and my grades only slightly better.

My dad said "Be an engineer.
Engineers make good money"

and I said "I'm terrible in math"

and he said "You have nice teeth
       and people like you."

True, my teeth were white as clouds
but the only people who liked me
were drunk old men and drunk teenagers.

This morning I stood in the parking lot
       of the slaughterhouse.

The biker was an okay guy.
He'd quit drinking liquor
and snorting powders
and was down to beer and weed.

He said "You in high school?"

I said "I'm in high school."

He said "That sucks."

The previous night, in the weeds, I kissed a girl
who stood well over six-feet tall
and, without being asked, lied
       about her weight
       ("like 138 pounds").
I asked her to take her top off
       but she'd said no
because we weren't far enough
from the keg and the other teenagers
       drinking warm beer

so I said we should keep walking
      deeper into the woods
      a mile, two miles
but we both knew the woods held snakes
      and poison ivy grew off the path
      so she jerked me off a little
and I squeezed her ass inside her jeans.

Back by the fire, she stumbled off
in her high-top sneakers
      giggling with a bunch of girls

and my friend said "Did you just fuck that pig?"

and I said "No"
      thinking, just thinking
maybe we should quit calling girls
      who let us touch them
            pigs.

Then I tried to kiss another girl
and she said "You just kissed that pig"

so I drank three more beers
in rapid succession
and passed out on a log.

      The next morning
      too sick to sleep

       I arrived early for work
       and accepted a beer
       from the biker
            a man twice my age.

I sipped the beer and it helped.

       The future I'd heard about for years
       felt more and more present
       though none of the faces I knew
       looked like maps:

not the half-drunk biker
who lived in a trailer
and bitched about child support
       not my dad losing his factory job
       as he approached 50 years old
not my mom who never wanted to work
       who wanted to stay at home
       long after her kids were gone
            who wept at her part-time jobs.

I wanted to be successful
       whatever that meant
but I didn't know how to be successful.

       No one knew how.

So I kept drinking
and felt successful

      as a drunk
      which I knew was a lie
      because the money going out
          was substantial
      but the money coming in
          was zilch
      and the chance to get laid
          was never as great as imagined.

The biker offered me another beer.

How do grown men
      with gray in their beards
end up working in a slaughterhouse
and living in aluminum boxes
and supporting kids they never see?

I took the beer.

The beer tasted warm and metallic
and turned my stomach like a wrench.

The biker said "You're not married?"

I said "I'm not married."

He said "I got kids but never wanted a wife."

The sun was out, a terrible orange.

## THE ABORTION PARTY

A boy knocked up a girl
and the girl didn't want the baby.
The boy didn't have the money
      for an abortion

so someone decided
      — one of the boy's friends
      or maybe the boy himself —
they should throw a field party
      get a couple kegs
          collect two bucks
          for every plastic cup
then use the money to pay for the abortion.

I thought that sounded like a great idea
      as far as terrible ideas go

because I knew about pregnancy
      the possibility of it
waiting for my girlfriend's period
waiting for another girl
who was not my girlfriend
      to get her period
waiting for a woman
who was 20 years older than me
      to get her period

talking my girlfriend into fucking
    while we waited for her period
hoping sex might shake something loose
    something like her period.

Word about the abortion party spread
and quickly became exaggerated —
plans were made, broken, made again
    kids were invited, uninvited, invited again.
Everybody wanted to get in on the fuckeduppedness.

The weekend came and instead all the guys
    worked or studied or hung out
    with their girlfriends
(the ones who weren't pregnant).

The next weekend came
    and the next.

    The party
without happening
without getting busted
without lacking in beer
    or drugs
    or hot chicks
    or muscle dudes
became legend.

Everyone claimed to have attended
        a party never thrown.

Then the pregnant girl
        either got her period
        or was never pregnant to begin with
        or her older sister came home from college
                and borrowed $300
                from someone
                to pay for the abortion.

The unborn child
        whatever we called it
        the fetus
        the problem
        the fucking disaster
stayed unborn
        like the boy's sperm
        never disappeared
        into the girl's body
        and touched an egg
then dripped down her thigh
in the backseat of a Camaro.

But there was the party we'd planned
        the idea of it
        the myth
and now we felt like we should blow it up.

I picked up Chris and headed to Beer World
	over in East Pittsburgh
	near the newly-defunct Eastland Mall
	and the bargain movie theater
	fronting the projects.

Outside, the parking lot held a flea market.
Inside, the closed Gimbels held a flea market.

At the flea markets, you could buy old magazines
	for a quarter
	or hot color TVs
	from the back of a truck.

The Beer World was going out of business.

We'd collected around $400
	in two-dollar increments
	with a few kids
kicking up a five or ten spot
	because they cared
	about the pregnant girl
	and the father-to-be
but now the abortion appeared unnecessary

	so Chris and I
like bankers in the vault afterhours
	scammed 100 off the top

>     filled my parents' car with gas
>     hit a drive-thru for burgers
> and generally acted like thieves.

Never has the prospect of new life
been more whimsical and useless
>     than with the people
>     most wired to create it.

If the pregnancy was null
>     then it was safe to fuck again.
If it was safe to fuck again
>     we'd need to get lots of booze.

>     At Beer World
we bought beer from Canada in green bottles
>     with grizzly bears on the labels.
>     We bought Dutch beer
>     and beer from Mexico.

Chris said "Stroh's?"
>     our usual swill
and held up a 30 pack.

Having more cheap stuff
was better than having not enough
>     expensive stuff

so we loaded up on Stroh's

then grabbed cases of 40s
>    malt liquor so powerful
>    they named it after a gun
>    named it after a venomous snake
>    named it after a deadly storm.

We bought wine coolers for the girls.
>    The girls would love us for wine coolers.

We bought bags of ice, cups by the sleeve.

Our cart filled like a bar fills on the weekend
>    and we rolled
>    giddy as cheerleaders
>    through the aisles
>    snagging daiquiri mix
>        margarita mix
>    bloody mary mix
because somewhere my older brother
bought vodka at the State Store
>    rotgut he'd overcharge us for
and the girls would love us for that, too —
>    paying money for fancy drinks
>    to get them drunk enough
>    to do the things they wanted to
>    and were embarrassed by.

That night turned into the day
>    turned into the next night.

The field turned into a motel room
    turned into a car on a backroad.

My parents didn't know where I was
    then they did
        then I was gone again.

    Every girl I kissed
    I begged to enter
    and every girl I entered
        I treated
        like a motel room
        I'd never rent again.

The party ended
    some version of it
without arrest or incident
    not even a fight
just drinking and fucking and dancing
    a big fire in a circle of rocks
and we went back to school
    to our parents
        to our part-time jobs.

    At work
we counted the time off in minutes
until the minutes became hours

       but with sex
the counting didn't start
          until the 31$^{st}$ day
          and by the 60$^{th}$ day
the numbers were unbearable.

I read all of the tracts the Christians passed out
        and the pamphlets from inside the clinic.

Inside, the nurse wouldn't talk to me
        just the girl.

I didn't understand how I'd ever been born.

## HAPPY

Happy to be off work on Friday night.
Happy to rent *Above the Law*
    starring Steven Seagal as Nico
    a Chicago cop who kicked a lot of ass
    using martial arts
        and a wrestling move
        called the clothesline
        where he smashed
        bad guys' throats
        with his forearm.
Happy Pam Grier starred as Nico's partner, Jacks
who also kicked a lot of ass
and looked sexy doing it
with her afro and super-solid tits —
    happy to think I could fight
        like Nico
    and maybe bang Jacks.

Happy to watch *Beaches*
    my girlfriend's choice
starring Bette Midler
    doing I-can't-remember-what
and singing "Wind Beneath My Wings"
which made my girlfriend cry
and push into me and I held her
and we pulled up a blanket.
My parents slept upstairs

while my girlfriend lifted her skirt
and tucked her panties in her purse.
Happy I had on sweatpants and no underwear.
>   Happy she was on the pill.
Happy not to come on the black fuzzy couch.
Happy to not have to scrub out any stains.
>   Not happy to drop off my girl at midnight.
>   Not happy to drive away with a hard-on
>   and her lipstick smeared on my mouth.

But happy to skip work
at the slaughterhouse on Saturday.
>   I slept in. I ate cereal. I watched cartoons
>   like I was nine and no one noticed.
Happy my dad gave me twenty bucks for no reason.

Not happy to go to church on Sunday
but happy to eat the chopped steak
at the Ponderosa in North Versailles
>   after the service.

Happy to study for Chemistry and understand
>   what I was studying
because I hadn't studied in a year.
>   Happy to have time to study.
My dad said "No work this weekend?"
>   and I said "No work this weekend."

Happy to be out of bed early on Monday
>   and off to the bus stop

where I bought everyone Cokes
from the convenience store.

At school, I made my seat before first bell.
    I studied in homeroom.
    In homeroom
    my teacher said
"Aren't you suddenly a serious student?"
    My homeroom teacher
        was happy
    I'd soon go back to failing.

Happy to give twenty dollars to a dude
    whose big brother would buy
    two cases of malt liquor
    in green hand-grenade bottles.

I paid attention during
    first, second, and third period.

Fourth-period lunch, I was out of money and happy.

Happy to ace the Chemistry test next period
and write my answers on the desk
so Larry Patton could copy and not fail —
    Larry Patton
    who looked like he studied at Harvard
    but did not study at all

      Larry Patton
      who did not work two part-time jobs
      Larry Patton
      who always had money and beer
      and was a blast to be around
      Larry Patton
      who moved to Colorado
      to instruct beautiful women
      on how to ski

while I went to college
    to be happy
or make my parents happy
or to learn how to get a good job
because money makes us happy
    all of us —
you can't get anything without cash
    not a job on a snowy mountain
        not a job teaching high school
maybe your ass kicked by a Chicago cop
and his hot-as-hell partner
    but even then
    you'd have to have had money
    to buy the drugs to smuggle
and who really wants to pay for that?
    Not me, and sure as fuck not Bette Midler.

## OUR FATHERS

were broke and out of work
and wore ties to interviews
where they didn't know what to say
    to other men in ties
    who'd read
*How to Win Friends & Influence People*
    and paid $100
    for the self-improvement seminar
    down at the convention center.

Our fathers skipped the convention center
and dragged us to Three Rivers Stadium
to watch the Pirates get slammed in nine innings.

Our fathers tried to balance the checkbook
    in ways that allowed
    for five days at the beach
    and school clothes.

Our fathers were alcoholics and heavy drinkers
    born-again Christians and habitual liars.
    They worked as insurance salesmen
        electricians, ambulance drivers
        pharmaceutical sales reps
        cooks and bartenders
        store managers and line supervisors
            factory grunts.

They were former bar owners
    who'd lost bars to drink.

They were wife-beaters, great cheaters, teetotalers
    big-time Catholics, Protestants who tithed.

    They shoveled snow
    from their neighbors' driveways
    when their neighbors turned
    too old to shovel snow.

    In interviews our fathers said
        "Well, I guess so"
    and shrugged at men with MBAs
        who asked
    "What are your strengths?"

Our fathers had more interviews
    for worse jobs
    and still they went.

Our fathers were ex-jocks
    who wanted football scholarships
    to big-time universities for their sons.
They were high school graduates
    or GED certificate earners
    trade school standouts
    army veterans who did not talk.

They threw hammers that whizzed by
      their children's heads
      took off their belts to make a point
      kicked ass from their favorite recliner
      knew the difference between
      a punch and a backhand
      and thought daily of choking their wives

      and oh how they loved us all!

They loved us in the morning
      over coffee and silence
          at night over beer
              on the weekend
                with a job to do—
the grass, the shrubs, the fence to paint.

They loved us with homes made of bricks
      backyards, balls, bats, shoes
      endless groceries, new used bicycles
      and the desire to get away
      keys to cars with V8 engines
      a neighborhood where you wouldn't get shot
      and they said "Go the fuck to school!"
      and they said "Go the fuck to school!"

Now they grow old and tired and mellow
    and say "I love you"
        and wait endlessly to be touched.

Fathers, you have nothing to be ashamed of.
    You probably did not beat us enough.

## TAKE ANTHONY DAVIS
## OUT OF THE HOLDING CELL

and walk him past the police desk
and unwrite the paperwork
and put him inside his car
and return him to the bar
and unpour every beer he hammered
and shot he slammed
and backstep him to the bathroom
to untoot all the blow
he stuffed up his nose
with his dirty-ass fingernail.
Reverse him home until the game on TV
is a sport not worth betting
and the child in the other room
is not listening for the fight
his dad and his mom have
every Friday night over football.
Do this again and again until
the bookies and drug dealers disappear
and the jobs and the money reappear
and do it again, holding down
the button of remorse for years and years
until the pain caused and accumulated
is as small as a strip of asphalt
        as small as a backboard and a hoop
        as small as the ball in Anthony Davis's hand
        as he skies for what feels like
        the best two points of his life.

His mother is in the window.
His father is at work.

There must be a way to do this right.

## THEY GROW UP

He grows up to be a lawyer and answers the phone
    at three AM to give free legal advice
    to a drunk friend he hasn't seen in 20 years.

Or he grows up to be a cook in a diner
    and steals cheese to feed his kids.

He grows up to be a professor
    at an online university and writes "Great!"
    and "Fantastic!" in the margins
    of all his students' terrible papers.

He drives a BMW.
He drives a Mercedes.
He drives a Ford Focus
    with 128,000 miles
    four bald tires
    and a crack in the windshield.

He grows up to be a writer
and changes everyone's name, mostly.

Or he deals drugs in Florida and bangs
    cross-dressing prostitutes from Haiti.

He works as a state cop and ignores all laws
    when it comes to his friends.

He marries his high school sweetheart.
He divorces his high school sweetheart.

He marries a woman with an Ivy League education
      who doesn't believe his stories
      about driving blind drunk
      on Pennsylvania backroads.

He marries a woman who teaches water aerobics
      to senior citizens.

He marries a real estate agent.
He starts selling real estate.

He sells drugs for a major pharmaceutical company.
      He deals blow.

He kills a man on a crack binge
      and hides the body under the bed.

He writes a letter to an old friend in jail
      doing 30 years on a murder rap.

He grows up to be a social worker
      and constantly complains about the stress.

He gets a great job managing an auto plant
      and coaches midget wrestling.

He wishes his son wrestled.
He wishes he still wrestled.

His daughter dances.
His daughter plays drums
      and loses the talent show
      to a dude on a pogo stick.
His daughter joins the Peace Corps
      for two years and moves to Burma.

He drinks 24 beers in 12 hours
      and stumbles from a boardwalk bar.
He drinks five shots in another bar
      before they cut him off
      then gets 86'd in another.
He gets arrested in New Jersey
      for driving drunk and calls his lawyer friend
      from high school, who wasn't a lawyer then
           just a nice smart kid
           who drank a lot of beer
           and maybe, at this hour
                would be willing to help.

## POEM FOR MR. VALLANO

An old man even then, already going gray
but you were stunningly handsome
sitting on the front porch steps
     soaked in sweat
     still in your jogging clothes
drinking a brown can of Schaefer beer.

All your children loved you.

## STACEY NEVER PROMISED ME A RODEO CHAMPIONSHIP
*-for B.K. and in memory of Marvin Malone*

"What are you talking about?" I said
and went back to the trick I was doing
with a carving knife, five fingers
and the wooden table in the breakroom.

    Billy repeated
"I think I want to be a cop after college"

        and the blade nicked the tip
        of one of my spread-out fingers.

What the hell was he talking about? Cop?
College? We hadn't even taken our SATs yet.

I'd just given up my dream of playing pro football
and was leaning towards rock band lyricist
        a job I imagined making me rich
        off the poems I'd been writing
        in spiral notebooks

        though I wouldn't read any real poetry
            until I was 21
            at the University of Pittsburgh
            mostly drunk and bored
            and angry and worried

about graduating and getting a job
when a professor gave me a book of factory poems

then all I wanted to do was read and write
    and not worry about graduating
    or getting a job

while Billy
    smart and straight-edged
finished school with a solid 3.0 GPA
in political science
and headed off to the Police Academy.

College was a joke but I finished
    dipping into textbooks
    when I wasn't reading Baudelaire
    who said "One should always be drunk"
    exactly what I wanted to hear
    exactly how I wanted to live
    exactly what I wanted to write

    so I did

and I published a poem in the *Wormwood Review*
    the most important poetry magazine
        in America
where Bukowski sent reams of his best poems
    and Williams S. Burroughs
    the great Gerald Locklin

>    William Wantling
>    before he destroyed himself
>        on booze, drugs, war, lies
>    and d.a. levy
>    from the Cleveland underground
>        before the cops arrested him
>        for reading indecent poems.

We all grow up — amazing
since most of my memories are cluttered with work.
The slaughterhouse was such a dungeon
    I couldn't imagine a future
    though Billy obviously did.

Later, when I was making four-plus bucks an hour
working at a shitty B. Dalton Bookstore
Billy was bringing home 28 grand plus benefits

        and right after that
        Marvin Malone
who edited the *Wormwood Review*
took four more of my poems and died.
        What a loss, that man and his magazine:
he took poets from around the country
and put their dangerous writings in a safe place
for other people who needed some danger
            to be inspired by.
    I still miss reading
    Mr. Malone's short generous letters

      and how he validated my dreams
      when my dreams were a joke
      to most of my friends and family

      and I remember being drunk with Billy
at the Rialto Bar in Greensburg
and how we talked about Jack Kerouac
and how Billy was ready to finish up
      at the Academy
      and move on to guns and badges
and how I was still lost on poetry but happy about it

and Billy said proudly "I write"

      and I said "Show me something"

and he did

and I told him to send it to the *Wormwood Review*

and he didn't

      but he sent me another poem called
      "Stacey Never Promised Me
            A Rodeo Championship"
an amazing work about a love triangle:
the man loved one woman
but slept violently with another

and I thought it was better than anything
by Louise Gluck who'd won the Pulitzer
for poems boring enough to blind readers.

Then everyone's lives changed again and forever
      each of us disappearing
         like smoke from car tires
      spinning on black asphalt.

I hope Marvin Malone is in poetry heaven
         publishing
      the angelic version of the *Wormwood Review*

and the last time I talked to Billy was 15 years ago
when I got arrested for drunk driving and wondered
how long it would take to lose my license
and he was still sweet and kind
      and not arresting poets.

That December he sent me a postcard
      saying "Call more often!"

which I meant to
      but didn't

though I still might
once I find the space
to write everything on my mind

and I keep thinking about another night at the Rialto
when I was drunk and bragging up Billy's poem
and I told him I'd steal it someday
    if he didn't publish it

so now I'd like to
    in honor of the poet
        who became a police officer
            who wrote the lines:

"Stacey never promised me a rodeo championship
but at least she let me be a cowboy once in a while."

# Acknowledgements

Thanks to the editors who published some of these poems in the following magazines, usually in different forms and with different titles: *Bender*, *Chiron Review*, *LA Cultural Weekly*, *Nerve Cowboy*, *Tears In The Fence* (UK), and *Wormwood Review*.

Also, special thanks to Ed Ochester and Judy Vollmer for featuring many of these poems in an issue of *5AM* with the author on the cover.

And finally, extra props to Lou Ickes for the use of his brilliant painting for the cover.

Made in the USA
Columbia, SC
22 September 2021